Disney Junior
Fancy NANCY

LONG ... OUT OF
Seattle Public Library

Nancy and the Mermaid Ballet

NewHolly Library

NOV 1 7 2020

Adapted by Nancy Parent
Based on the episode written by Matt Hoverman
Illustrated by the Disney Storybook Art Team

HARPER

An Imprint of HarperCollinsPublishers

Copyright © 2020 by Disney Enterprises, Inc.
All rights reserved. Manufactured in China.
No part of this book may be used or reproduced in any manner whatsoever without written permission except
in the case of brief quotations embodied in critical articles and reviews. For information address
HarperCollins Children's Books, a division of HarperCollins Publishers, 195 Broadway, New York, NY 10007.
www.harpercollinschildrens.com

ISBN 978-0-06-298333-6

20 21 22 23 24 SCP 10 9 8 7 6 5 4 3 2 1 ❖ First Edition

Ooh la la! Today we are having tryouts for the Mermaid Ballet. Bree and I both want to play the lead part of the mermaid. But I am the only dancer who brought her own mermaid crown.

"Bravo!" cries Madame Lucille. "You all did very well. Let's take a break while I assign parts!"

"How'd you do?" asks Bree.

"Not to brag, but *magnifique*!" I tell her. "How will Madame Lucille ever decide between us? What if she makes us both mermaids?"

"Yes, that's perfect!" says Bree.

"And now for the moment you've all been waiting for . . ."
says Madame Lucille.

She reads the list. Bree and I are shocked. Neither of us
got the part.

"How did the big audition go?" Dad asks
when we get home.
"I'm an oyster," says Bree.
"I'm slimy seaweed!" I say.

"Dad, it's even worse than you know," I say.

Then Grace rides by.

"Hi, Mr. and Mrs. Clancy," she says. "Did you hear? I'm the mermaid!"

"Let us go far away from here . . . to a place that will help us forget we ever wanted to be mermaids," I say to Bree.

We go to the backyard, where I had already set up for a fancy mermaid tea party to celebrate.

"I was sure one of us would get the part," I tell her.

"I guess I'm kind of hungry," says Bree.

"Even though I really wanted the role, I would have been so happy for you if you got it," says Bree. "And I would have been more than happy for you. I would have been elated!" I say.

Bree and I go to ballet class the next morning. Everyone is whispering.

"Didn't you hear?" asks Jonathan. "Grace fell off her bike and sprained her ankle. She can't dance."

"Who's going to be the mermaid?" I ask.

Madame Lucille is about to tell us, so I grab my mermaid crown from my ballet bag.

"I better be prepared," I say.

"Grace is fine," says Madame Lucille. "She'll stay in the show as a clam. And the part of the mermaid will go to Bree!"

"Can you believe it?" Bree asks me excitedly.

Magnifique!

Bonjour!

The Fancier the Better!

Sacrebleu!

Ooh la la!

© 2020 Disney Enterprises, Inc.

"Not really," I say, disappointed. But then I tell my best friend, "Congratulations!" That's fancy for I'm happy for you.

The class is happy for Bree too.

I slip the mermaid crown back into my bag.

We start to learn our parts for the ballet.

Rhonda and Wanda are seahorses.

Lionel moves
like a shark.

Grace opens and
closes like a clam.

As I sway and move closer to Bree, I tell Madame Lucille I've been working on my character's story.

"You see, I'm no ordinary seaweed," I say. "I'm seaweed that dreams of being a mermaid!"

"Uh, seaweed, stay in the back, please," Madame Lucille says. "You're anchored to the sea floor."

On the ride home, Bree tries to cheer me up.
"You may not be the mermaid, but I know you're
gonna be the best strand of seaweed ever!" she says.
But Bree just doesn't understand.

After Bree gets out of the car, Mom asks me if everything is all right.

"No," I say, running into the house. "Things are bad, terrible, horrendous! I'm quitting the Mermaid Ballet!"

Mom comes up to my room to ask what's wrong.

"Ever since Bree got the mermaid part, she's impossible!" I tell her. "I should be happy for her, but instead I feel . . ."

"Jealous?" asks Mom.

"*Excusez-moi?* Me? Jealous?" I say. That's fancy for feeling bad when someone else gets something nice.

"*Sacrebleu!* Oh no!" I say. "I am jealous. Oh, I'm such a bad friend."

"It's natural to feel a little jealous," says Mom. "I bet if you give it a little time, the feeling will melt away."

Suddenly I hear music playing. I grab Marabelle so we can look out my window. Bree is practicing in her room.

"Marabelle," I say. "Look how well Bree is dancing. She was meant to be the mermaid."

I have an idea! I grab something and run to Bree's house.

"*Bonjour*, Bree," I say. "I'm sorry I was weird before. I wanted to be happy for you, but I was jealous. You're such a good dancer, you deserve to be the mermaid. And you deserve this too."

"Oh, Nancy, thank you," says Bree. "This will really help. I'm a little nervous to be the mermaid. There are so many steps!"

"You're going to be brilliant," I say. "You're going to practice. And I'll be swaying behind you every step of the way!"